Left and Right with
ANT and BEE

written and illustrated by Angela Banner

EGMONT

This **ANT and BEE** book

belongs to

. . . .

One day Ant and Bee were just
about to fly to the library . . .

. . . when Ant said NO!

Ant said it was his turn
to carry Bee.

Ant said he would carry
Bee to the library.

LEFT

RIGHT

But Ant walked very slowly

Then Bee
said Ant could
not carry him
any more!

So Ant said he
would pull Bee
to the library
on a big leaf.

Bee told Ant that the way
to the library was LEFT . . .
but Ant went RIGHT.

Then Ant pulled Bee over
lots of stones.

BUMP! BUMP! BUMP!

...ee had a bath.

Then Bee bandaged up all his bumps.

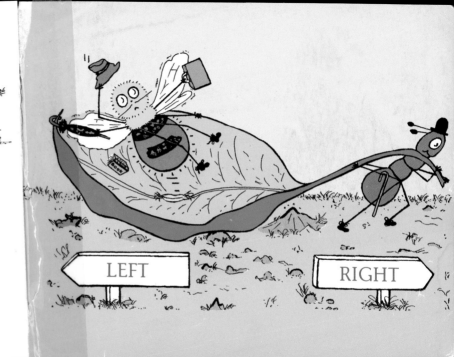

LEFT

RIGHT

Then Bee got cross.

Poor Bee had mud all over his
body and Bee had bumps too.

Bee said he did not want
to be carried or pulled by
Ant any more.

. . . inside the little old motor car.

Then Ant and Bee put the little

old motor car inside a garage.

Then Ant and Bee flew

LEFT to the library.

Which way is Ant pointing

with his stick?

Bee had a bath.

Then Bee
bandaged up
all his bumps.

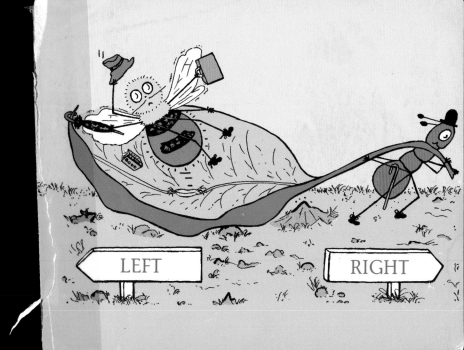

LEFT

RIGHT

Then Bee got cross.

Poor Bee had mud all over his body and Bee had bumps too.

Bee said he did not want to be carried or pulled by Ant any more.

Bee said he did not
want to be carried
or pulled by Ant
any more . . .

. . . and Ant said
he did not want
to fly with Bee.

Ant and Bee were sad because they could not go to the library together because Bee would not walk.

Then Ant went away to think
how to take Bee to the library.

Suddenly Ant saw . . .

. . . a little old motor car.

No one wanted the little old
motor car . . . so Ant drove
away in the little old motor
car to find Bee.

HONK! HONK! TOOT! TOOT!

Bee was in a toy shop!

Bee had made all his bumps better and Bee had made himself happy by looking at toys.

Suddenly Bee heard a loud noise! HONK! HONK! TOOT! TOOT!

The loud noise was the horn
on the little old motor car!

Ant said he had found
a little old motor car for Bee.

Now Bee need not fly . . .
or be carried or pulled, because
now Ant could drive Bee
to the library.

Bee got inside the little old
motor car and asked Ant
to drive him to the library.

HONK! HONK! TOOT! TOOT!

OFF went Ant and Bee in the
little old motor car on their way
to the library.

HONK
HONK

TOOT
TOOT

Ant SLOWED,
STOPPED,
LOOKED
and LISTENED.
Then Ant
said, "Off I go,
safe and slow."

The way to the library was LEFT

. . . but which way has Ant gone?

34

Bee was busy reading his book
so Bee did not see that Ant was
NOT going to the library.

Ant and Bee and the little old
motor car were going to . . .

... a  FUNFAIR

It was a big, noisy funfair so
Bee said they would go to the
library after they had played
at the funfair.

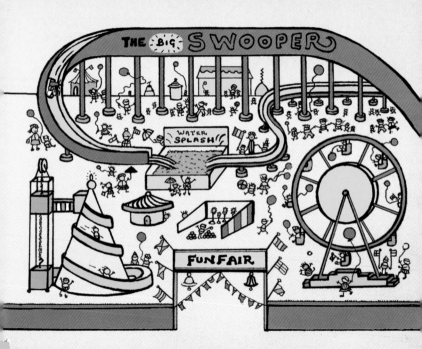

LEFT

YELLOW
RINGS
← THIS WAY

HOOPLA

Which way must
Bee throw his rings?

RED RINGS RIGHT
THIS WAY →

HOOPLA

MUSIC BOX

Which way must
Ant throw his rings?

LEFT

TO THE
ROCKET
RIDES

Then Bee called Ant to come
and drive him to the library.
HONK! HONK! TOOT! TOOT!

OFF went Ant and Bee in the
little old motor car on their
way to the library.

Ant SLOWED,
STOPPED,
LOOKED
and LISTENED.
Then Ant
said, "Off I go,
safe and slow."

The way to the library was LEFT

. . . but which way has Ant gone?

Bee was playing with his prize so Bee did not see that Ant was NOT going to the library.

Ant and Bee and the little old motor car were going to . . .

... a BOAT POND.

It was a very busy boat pond
so Bee said they would go to the
library after they had played
on the water.

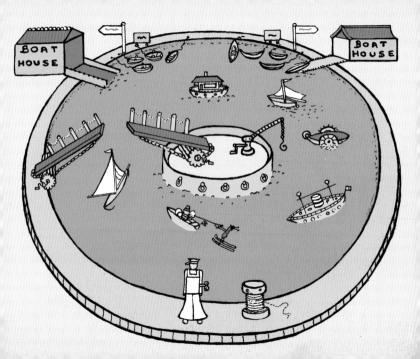

Which way must Bee go?

Which way must Ant go?

Ant and Bee played on the water until night-time.

Then Bee said they must go to sleep on a boat called a houseboat.

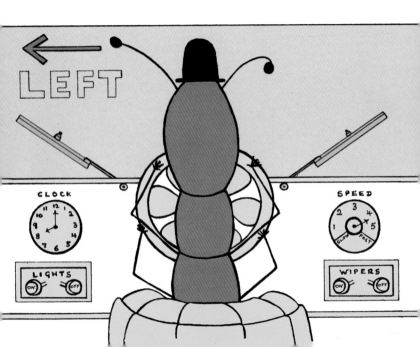

On the next day Bee wrote LEFT on the little old motor car to remind Ant that the way to the library was LEFT.

HONK! HONK! TOOT! TOOT!

Suddenly it began to rain
and the rain washed off the red
arrow and the word LEFT .

CLOCK

Ant SLOWED,
STOPPED,
LOOKED
and LISTENED.
Then Ant
said, "Off I go,
safe and slow."

The way to the library was LEFT

. . . but which way has Ant gone?

Bee was playing with his boats
so Bee did not see that Ant was
not going to the library.

Ant and Bee and the little old
motor car were going to . . .

. . . a FARM

It was a clean and happy farm
so Bee said they would go to the
library after they had played at
the farm.

Which way will Bee go?

Which way will Ant go?

LEFT

THIS WAY TO
THE BABY
RABBITS

Then Bee called Ant to come
and drive him to the library.
HONK! HONK! TOOT! TOOT!

OFF went Ant and Bee in the
little old motor car on their
way to the library.

Ant SLOWED,
STOPPED,
LOOKED
and LISTENED.
Then Ant
said, "Off I go,
safe and slow."

The way to the library was LEFT

. . . but which way has Ant gone?

Bee was playing with his straw and his horseshoe so Bee did not see that Ant was not going to the library.

Ant and Bee and the little old motor car were going to . . .

. . . the SEASIDE .

It was lovely by the seaside so
Bee said they would go to the
library after they had played at
the seaside.

SEASIDE

Which way will Bee go?

Which way will Ant go?

Ant and Bee played at the
seaside until night-time.

Then Bee said they must sleep
in a tent on the beach.

On the next day Bee made Ant wear LEFT-hand gloves with LEFT-hand finger labels to remind Ant to turn LEFT to the library.

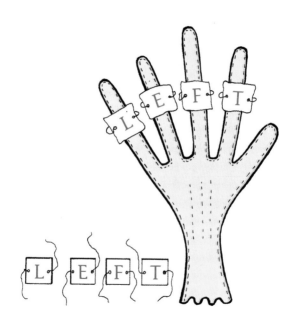

BUT Ant waved both LEFT hands and all his LEFT-hand finger labels fell off and Bee did not see.

Ant SLOWED,
STOPPED,
LOOKED
and LISTENED.
Then Ant
said, "Off I go,
safe and slow."

The way to the library was LEFT

... but which way has Ant gone?

Bee was playing with his shells so Bee did not see that Ant was NOT going to the library.

Ant and Bee and the little old motor car were going to . . .

. . . an AIRPORT

It was an exciting AIRPORT
so Bee said they would go to the
library after they had played at
the AIRPORT.

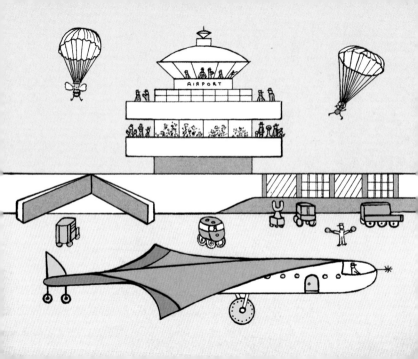

Which way must Bee go?

Which way must Ant go?

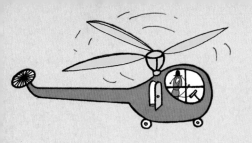
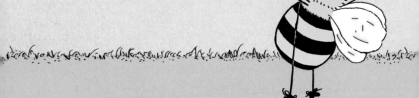

Then Bee called
Ant to come and
drive him to the
library BUT Ant
said his feet were
tired of motor
car driving.

Then Ant said he wanted
to fly to the library . . . BUT
NOT BY AEROPLANE!

Ant said he wanted to fly
to the library . . . with BEE.

Then Bee was very happy.

Then Ant and Bee put all

these things . . .